For Max Lerman —S.C.

For Bailey—
whose every sound and movement
is a joyful jazz in our memories
—B.D.

JAZZMATAZZ!

By Stephanie Calmenson

Illustrated by Bruce Degen

HarperCollins Publishers

When the weather gets cold
And a mouse slips in,
A jazzmatazz story
Is sure to begin.

You won't hear a bell
Or a knock at the door.
The mouse will come in
Through a crack in the floor.

While you're washing the dishes,
He'll step on your feet,

Then scurry in a hurry
To the piano seat.

You'll scoot him away,
But he's got pizzazz.
He jumps on the keys . . .

And starts to play jazz!

Doo-dat, diddy-dat,
Diddy-dat, doo!

"I plink, *plink*, plink.
How about you?"

Mouse points to Dog,
With his bones and bowl.

"I play my drum with
My heart and soul!"

Doo-dat, diddy-dat,
Diddy-dat, doo!

"I bang-a-bang, bang!
How about you?"

Dog points to Cat,
Who says, "It's no riddle.

You know what *I* play.
I'm the cat with the fiddle."

Doo-dat, diddy-dat,
Diddy-dat, doo!

"I fiddle-dee-dee.
How about you?"

Cat points to Bird,
Who sings, "Tweetily-tweet.
My voice is my music.
Isn't it sweet?"

Doo-dat, diddy-dat,
Diddy-dat, doo!

"I tweetily-tweet.
How about you?"

Bird points to Fish,
Who swims round and round.
"My itty bitty bubbles
Make a blub-blub sound."

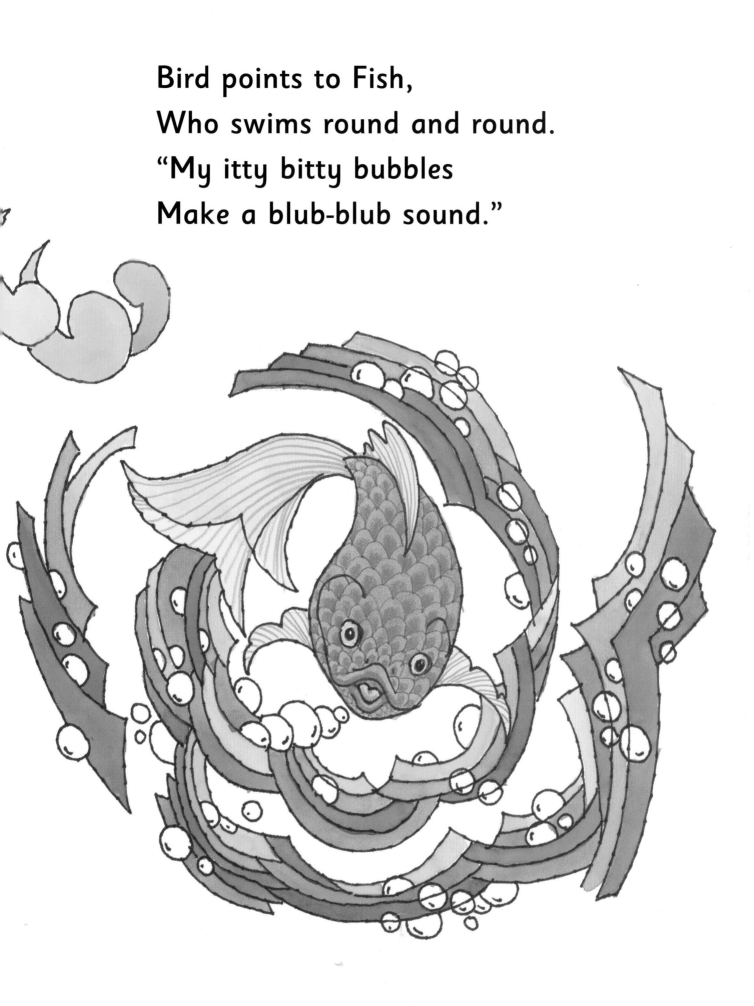

When Fish points to me,
Here's what I say,

"I love to sing and
There's plenty that I play!"

"But my feet are tapping
And they just won't stop.
Will you look at me now?

I'll tap till I drop!"

Doo-dat, diddy-dat,
Diddy-dat, doo!
"I tap-tap-tapitty.
How about you?"

Come on, everybody.
It's time to join in!
Our jazzmatazz jamming
Will now begin.

Plink, plink.
Bang-a-bang.
Fiddle-dee-dee.
Tweetily-tweet.
Blub-blub.
Tap with me!

Doo-dat, diddy-dat,

Diddy-dat, doo!

A Note from the Author and Artist

On a cold winter day, we were on e-mail, chatting about this and that. At some point, we got to talking about the weather.

Bruce: The field mice are coming into our house to get warm.

Stephanie: City mice do the same. I squeak—I mean, speak— from experience.

Bruce: Speaking of squeaking, last night a mouse ran across my foot while I was washing the dishes, then ran under the piano!

Stephanie: Train the mouse to run *on* the piano—and play *jazz*!

Bruce: Therein lies a children's book.

You are now holding that book in your hands.

Diddy-dat, doo!

STEPHANIE CALMENSON   BRUCE DEGEN

Jazzmatazz!
Text copyright © 2008 by Stephanie Calmenson
Illustrations copyright © 2008 by Bruce Degen

Manufactured in China.
Library of Congress Cataloging-in-Publication Data is available.
ISBN-10: 0-06-077289-1 — ISBN-13: 978-0-06-077289-5
ISBN-10: 0-06-077290-5 (lib. bdg.) — ISBN-13: 978-0-06-077290-1 (lib. bdg.)

Typography by Carla Weise   2 3 4 5 6 7 8 9 10   ❖   First Edition